PRESENTED TO

_____

FROM

_____

DATE

Also by Alice Boggs Lentz

Tweetsie Adventure

Mountain Magic

A Family's Legacy of Faith

ALICE BOGGS LENTZ

Illustrated by David Griffin

Tommy
NELSON™

Thomas Nelson, Inc.
Nashville

Now there are also many other things that Jesus did. Were every one of them to be written. I suppose that the world itself could not contain the books that would be written. John 21:21

the grass withers the flower fades But the word of god is forever

Legacy

of religious freedom

bequeath   our nation

a will to pass on   Peace of Justice & righteousness
            strength of heart, success of liberty

giust

Family Legacy   quest for the Holy Grail to search, seek to ask questions
such as ... finding out that my grandfathers T.B. was caused from shoveling coal into the furnace in the military working in 140° temp. that no compensation was given to my grandmother or family. "He was just doing his job."
            Walter Vincent Roberts

Unions blocked the roads & took jobs from small farmers

Age of 2 yr. Jenny fell in the fountain before she was on board for the USA from Sweden
            John   Pletscher
Holmberg   in France

Neta & Tena were the 9th & 10th children of Norwegian imagrents born in this country.   Jesus asked ... the crowd

Mountain Magic

Text copyright © 1998 by Alice Boggs Lentz.

Who do they say I am? JB, Elijah, one of the prophets from old risen

Illustrations copyright © 1998 by David Griffin.

Who do you say I am. Peter Luke 9:20

"He answered the Christos"

Blessed are you" Matt 16:17

Published in Nashville, Tennessee, by Tommy Nelson™, a division of Thomas Nelson, Inc. Executive Editor: Laura Minchew; Managing Editor: Beverly Phillips; Project Manager: Susan Ligon.

& but when Peter said in Matt 16:21-23 this shall never happen to you." Jesus "Far be it from you Lord replyed "Get behind me Satan, you are a hinderance" in the end Peter followed Jesus to death on the cross.

Library of Congress Cataloging-in-Publication Data
Lentz, Alice B.

"whoever looses his life for my sake will save it" Luke 9:23

Mountain magic / by Alice Boggs Lentz : illustrated by David Griffin.
    p.   cm.
    Summary: Recalls the lure of the mountains that first draws a family to spend the summer there in Grandmother's house and brings them back year after year even when the children are grown and have children of their own.
    ISBN 0-8499-5841-5

to Thomas Jesus said Do not be disobedient but believe. John 20:28, & Thomas answered My Lord & My God." 29

You have seen me? Blessed are those who have not seen

    [1. Mountain life—Fiction. 2. Family life—Fiction.
3. Christian life—Fiction.] I. Griffin, David, 1952- ill.
II. Title.
PZ7.L54235Mo   1998
[E]--dc21   98-11050
                                                CIP
                                                 AC

and yet believe," John 20:31

Jesus said Have you believed because

These are written so that you may believe that Jesus is the Christ the Son of God, and that by believing you may have life in his Name.

Printed in the United States of America

98 99 00 01 02 WCV 9 8 7 6 5 4 3 2 1

Malachi 3:7 returne to me & I will returne to you you will be a land of delight!

draw near to me & I will draw near to you James 4

above all these put on Love which binds everything together in perfect harmony. And let the peace of Christ rule in your hearts, to which indeed you were called in one body! And be thankful.

Thank you to my parents for all the moves made with confidence! to Dave's parents for the stability & friendships they formed for children to share with, garden with, grow with & Grandchildren to enjoy it all with who eat the fruit of labor. God be with us untill we meet again.

Ayla & Naomi, continue to sing "go tell it on the Mountain over the hill & everywhere. That Jesus Christ is born.

Who can climb the mountain & stand in the holy place. The one who has a clean heart who's sins have been erased. For your the generation and you'll receive a blessing from the God of Love & Grace. For your the generation of those who seek his face.

Lift up your heads O portals. Lift up, O ancient doors. The King of glory enters and reigns forever more.

Graeme add your story to you. Your mom Ruth tells you to pray like this... Thanks you god. Sorry god. Please god. T.S.P. a measure of faith true to her Name.

Great is thy faithfulness. Strength for today & bright hope for tomorrow.

FOREWORD

If you have been to the mountains,

you will enjoy this book in a special way.

If you haven't, this book will make you

want to come. It is very much like the place

where I live. I hope you enjoy reading it

as much as I have.

RUTH BELL GRAHAM

Acknowledgments by Alice Boggs Lentz:

My warmest thanks to all who made this book possible—

to my husband, who supports me;

to my family, for the gift of the story;

to friends, for their encouragement;

to the folks at Tommy Nelson, whose embrace I treasure;

to David Griffin, whose paintings make words sing;

and to Ruth Bell Graham, who, when I knocked,

    flung the door open wide.

Acknowledgments by David Griffin:

My sincere thanks to the following people for their help

throughout this project—

to Leslie Camp, for starting this whole process by introducing

    me to the Tommy Nelson family;

to Laura Minchew, who believed it would work and opened

    the door to a terrific opportunity;

to Susan Ligon, for supporting, encouraging and enabling

    me to see a dream come true;

to Alice Boggs Lentz, for sharing her family's story for the

    rest of us to be a part of;

and to Lorna, Ryan, Elizabeth, and Michael—my family,

    my life, that allowed the images to come to life.

One generation

shall praise thy works

to another,

and shall declare

thy mighty acts.

PSALM 145:4 KJV

The summer heat drove us up into the mountains. But it was the mountain magic that tugged at us to stay.

There were seven of us — Grandmother, Mama, Daddy, my three brothers, and me.

Grandmother was the first to tell us about the mountains. She told us about the green peaks that leap to the sky. She told us about the blue ridges that look like the ocean's waves. And she told us about the creek that flows near her house.

Early one morning that summer, we boarded the train to go to the mountains. The engine belched black smoke as it passed over the flat, cracked land. The cinders that blew in through the windows covered our faces and arms.

My throat felt parched and dry, like the corn fields we crossed. I just couldn't imagine what Grandmother was talking about.

By late afternoon, the train chugged uphill.
We left the heat behind, and suddenly everything
was green. The mountains smelled so cool.

Surely this is the way to heaven, I thought.

We rode in a wagon to Grandmother's house. The wagon carried us around a lake. On its glassy green surface were reflections of the mountain peaks.

Grandmother's house had eight rooms and a porch with rocking chairs. It had a bathtub with feet that looked like a lion's paws. There *always* were crickets in the bathtub.

But we didn't mind, because mostly we showered outside when it rained.

We heard the creek before
we could see it. Rushing water
drowned our squeals and laughter.
We slid down the bank and splashed
our feet in the liquid ice.

While in the mountains that summer, we played in the creek every day.

We learned to climb from rock to rock without getting our feet wet.

We learned to pick rhododendron blossoms without getting the sticky stuff on our hands.

We learned to make slingshots.

When I tested my aim on my brother's backside,
I learned just how angry Grandmother could be.

I told my brother I was sorry.

And for Mama and Grandmother, I picked the best
rhododendron blossoms I could find. They loved
them and put them in a vase inside the house.

While in the mountains that summer, we often took evening walks.

And always, always, before bed, we sat on the porch and sang hymns.
Our grown-ups insisted on it.

Our hymn-sings ended with the doxology: "Praise God from Whom all blessings flow. Praise Him, all creatures here below…."

I always thought, *We sound almost like angels.*

Every summer the mountain magic grabbed us
just as it had that first year.

Oh, sure, little things changed. We grew older and bolder.
Took longer hikes. Learned the second verses of hymns.

Daddy bought a 1937 Plymouth, and after that, we stopped
riding the train.

But the big things never changed. The creek still enchanted us. Our hymn-sings still sounded almost like angels' choirs.

And the mountains always refreshed our spirits.

One summer I brought my
sweetheart to the mountains.

Later he became my husband.

Later still, we all brought our children to the mountains. There they played with cousins and grew to love their aunts and uncles.

My sons made slingshots and built dams in the creek. My nieces learned to play the guitar, and our hymn-sings were forever changed.

And in time, another generation joined our song.

The mountain magic still tugs at my brothers and me.

The four of us gathered there one day last spring. We picnicked on a boulder in the creek where once as youngsters we had spent the night. We climbed from rock to rock without getting our feet wet.

We gave thanks for the blessings that have flowed through our lives like the creek through the mountains.

That evening, we sat on the porch in the familiar rocking chairs. Our voices blended in song.

". . . Praise Him above, ye heavenly host. Praise Father, Son, and Holy Ghost."

I just couldn't imagine that the angels themselves would have sung more beautifully.